T0000809

For Asha and Laurel. —C.S.

This book is dedicated to my parents,
my guiding lights and the center
of my universe. —R.W.

Text copyright © 2024 by Candace Savage
Illustrations copyright © 2024 by Rachel Wada

24 25 26 27 28   5 4 3 2 1

All rights reserved. No part of this book may be reproduced,
stored in a retrieval system or transmitted, in any form or by any means,
without the prior written consent of the publisher or a license from
The Canadian Copyright Licensing Agency (Access Copyright).
For a copyright license, visit accesscopyright.ca or call toll free to 1-800-893-5777.

Greystone Kids / Greystone Books Ltd.
greystonebooks.com

Cataloguing data available from Library and Archives Canada
ISBN 978-1-77164-843-1 (cloth)
ISBN 978-1-77164-845-5 (epub)

Editing by Kallie George
Copy editing by Elizabeth McLean and Tracy Bordian
Proofreading by Tracy Bordian
Expert review by geologist Michael Cuggy and astronomer
Dr. Daryl Janzen, University of Saskatchewan
Jacket and text design by Sara Gillingham Studio
The illustrations in this book were rendered digitally.

Printed and bound in Malaysia on FSC® certified paper at Papercraft.
The FSC® label means that materials used for the product have been responsibly sourced.

Greystone Books thanks the Canada Council for the Arts, the British Columbia Arts Council, the Province of British Columbia
through the Book Publishing Tax Credit, and the Government of Canada for supporting our publishing activities.

Greystone Books gratefully acknowledges the xʷməθkʷəy̓əm (Musqueam),
Sḵwx̱wú7mesh (Squamish), and səlilwətaɬ (Tsleil-Waututh) peoples on
whose land our Vancouver head office is located.

BY CANDACE SAVAGE · ILLUSTRATED BY RACHEL WADA

ALWAYS
BEGINNING

The Big Bang, the Universe, and You

GREYSTONE KIDS

GREYSTONE BOOKS · VANCOUVER / BERKELEY / LONDON

In the beginning everything
everything lay curled up tight:

the world inside its egg.

the universe tiny as a seed.

Crick, crack, the shell split,

the seed shattered: strangeness and wonder burst forth.

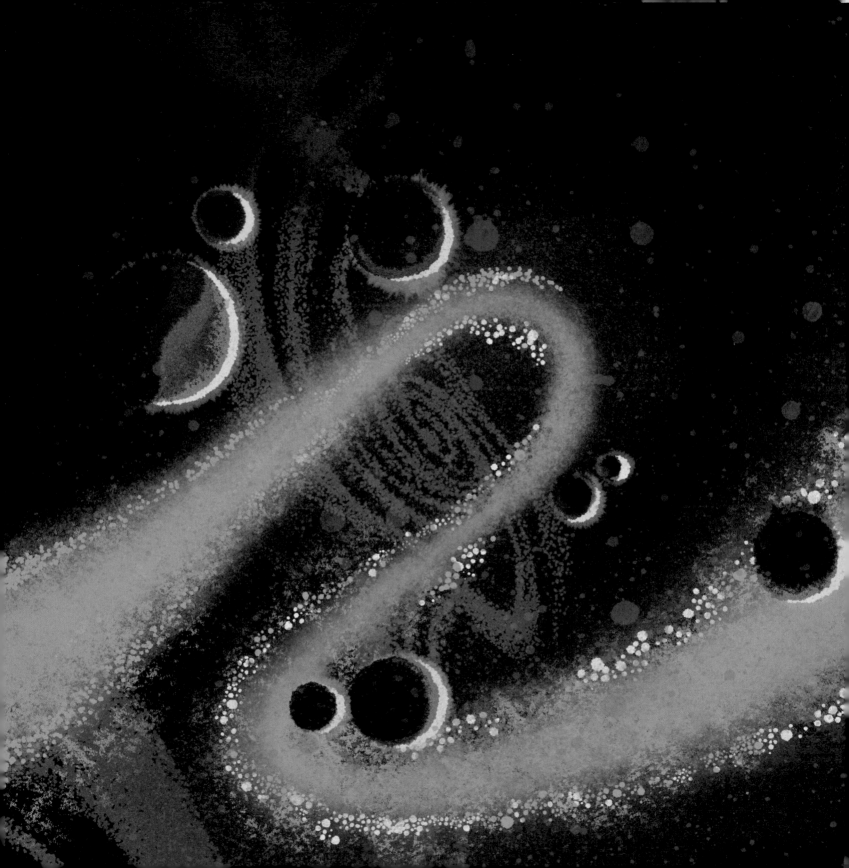

Sizzling stars spiralled into galaxies.

Stony planets cooled,
circled their chosen suns.

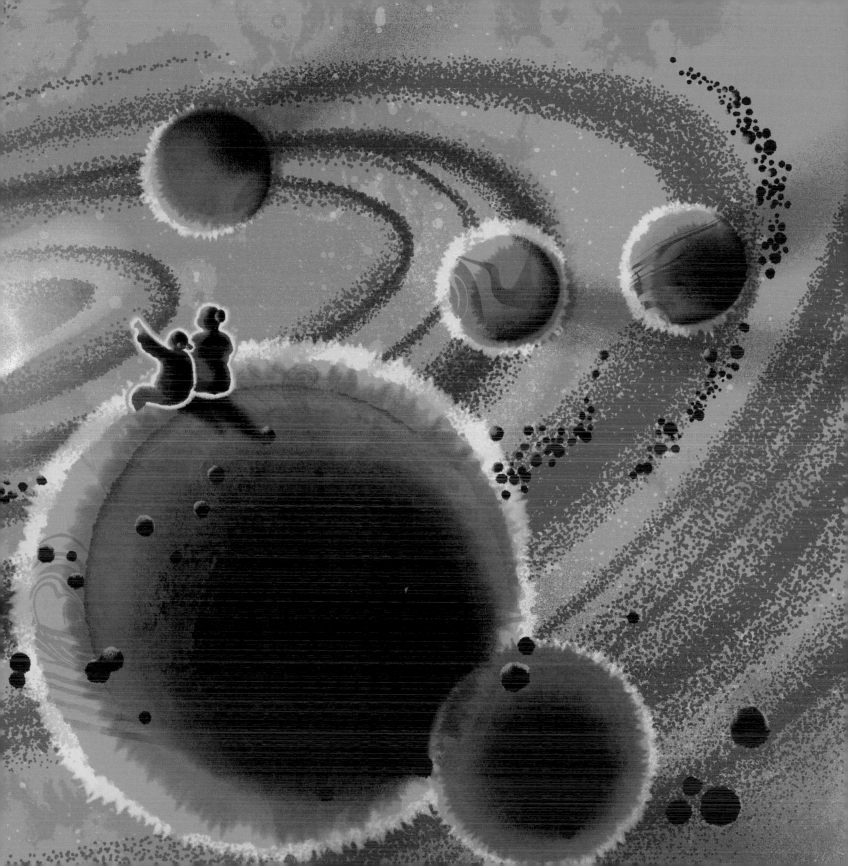

Blue water came from distant stars,

borne to Earth by icy messengers.

Planetesimals spiced the briny soup,

soon simmering with life!

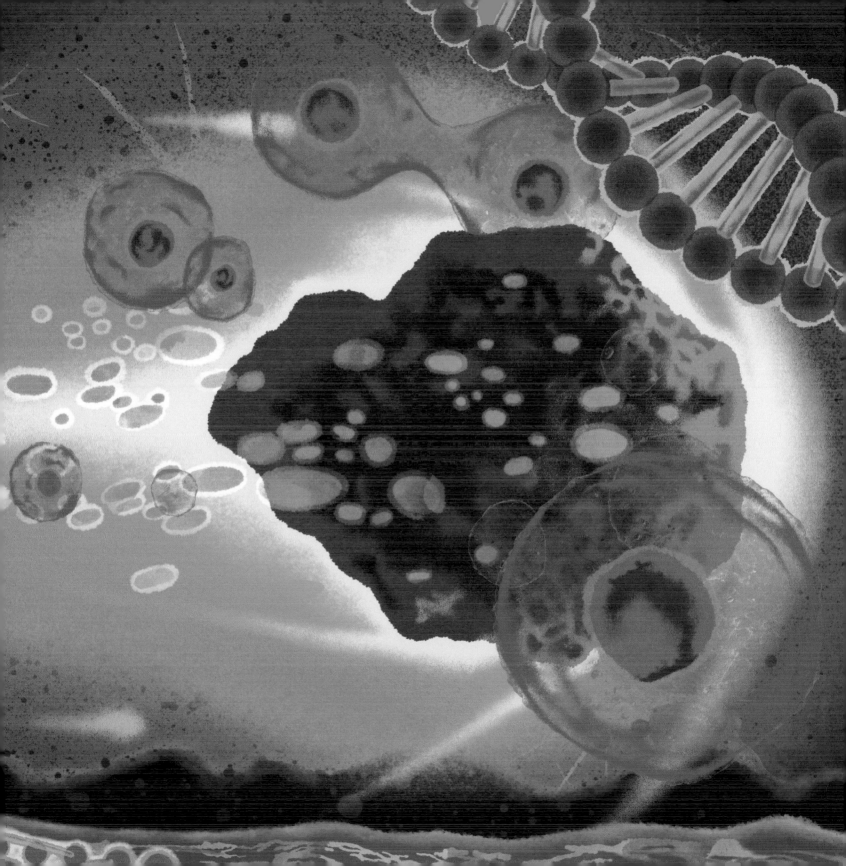

Life, sluggish

and slimy—

life, wriggly and writhing—

life, gnashing and gnarled—

in the salty sea

and on the new green land.

Everything everyone made of strangeness and wonder.

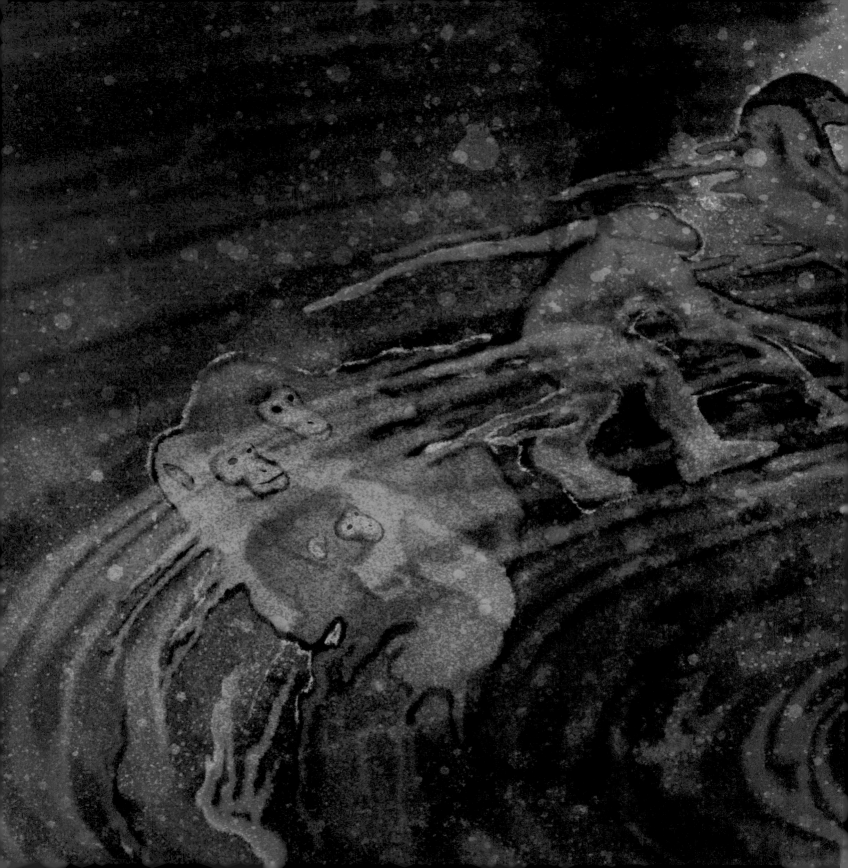

at home under these dancing stars.

Each new day holds tomorrow
tight in its arms:

an egg   a seed

everything   everything   always beginning.

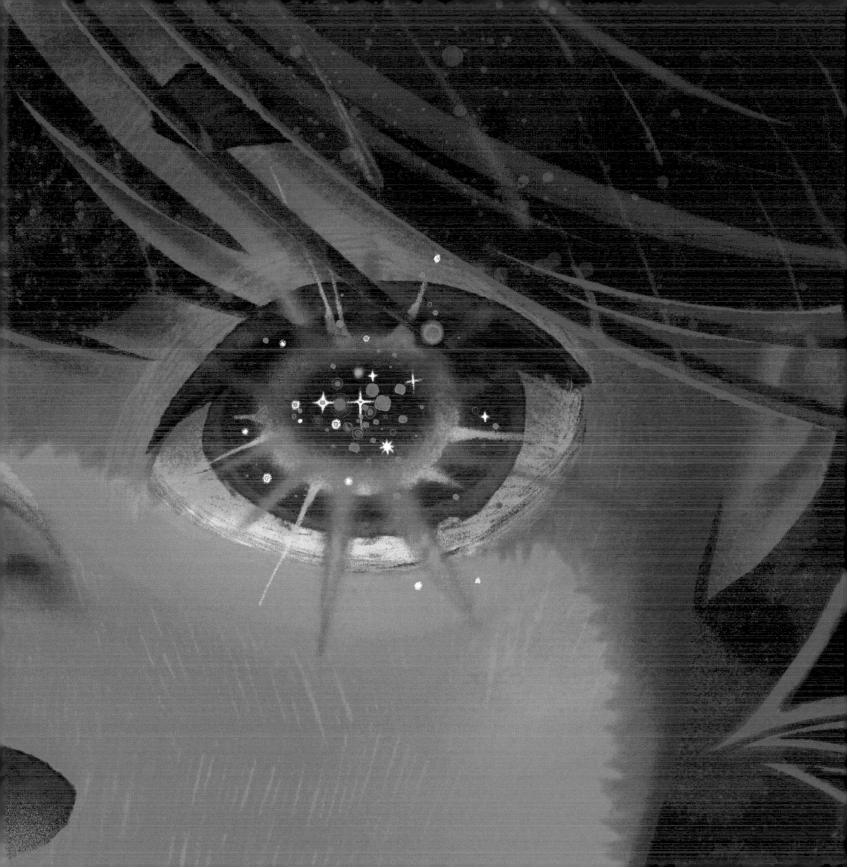

Timeline

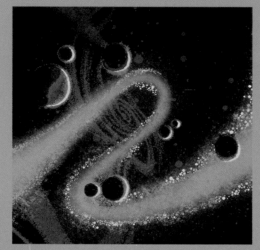

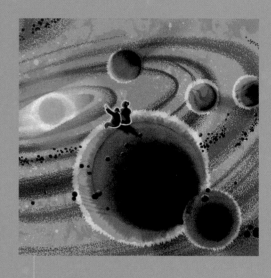

THE BIG BANG

Scientists think that long ago, everything in the universe was squeezed into a point smaller than the dot at the end of this sentence. Then, about 13.8 billion years ago, the universe suddenly began to expand. This explosive change is called the Big Bang.

STARS

The early universe was filled with clouds of gas and dust. Stars formed as these clouds collapsed and grew hot enough to glow. Gravity held the stars together in clusters, or galaxies.

PLANETS

Planets, including Earth, began to form about 4.6 billion years ago, when bits of space debris collided and stuck together. We live in a galaxy called the Milky Way, on the third planet out from a middle-sized star, our Sun.

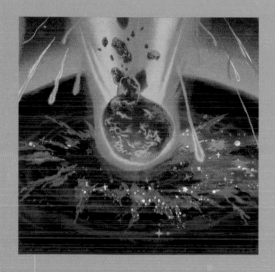

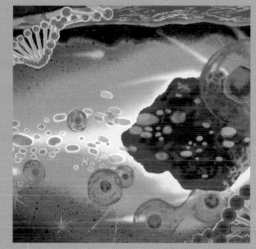

TINY LIVES

When comets and other planetesimals (small space objects) crashed into Earth, they brought the building blocks for life. The first living things were single cells, like bacteria and amoebas, that floated around in the ocean.

WATER

For a long time, Earth was stony and dry. Then, about 4.4 billion years ago, water began to pool on the surface, some of it brought from space by frozen ice balls, or comets.

PRECAMBRIAN ERA

Once begun, life slowly, slowly evolved into more complex forms. These strange, spongy seaweeds and boneless animals lived about 600 million years ago, in the Precambrian Era.

CAMBRIAN ERA

By about 500 million years ago, many new forms of ocean life had evolved. The seas of the Cambrian Era were teeming with shellfish, feathery sea anemones and five-eyed creatures with clawed snouts.

AGE OF FISHES

Enormous armored fish competed with the world's first sharks in the warm seas of the Devonian Period, about 400 million years ago. They were the first animals with backbones.

LAND ANIMALS

By 360 million years ago, four-limbed fish had dragged themselves out of the ocean to live on marshy land. These pioneers were the ancestors of all amphibians, reptiles and mammals.

AGE OF MAMMALS

When a huge meteor struck
Earth about 65 million years ago,
dinosaurs and many other species
became extinct. But mammals
began to thrive, including the first
bats, cats, dogs and elephants.
These animals lived in families
when their babies were young.

AGE OF REPTILES

Beginning about 250 million years
ago, dinosaurs and other reptiles
dominated a world alight with
flowers, bees, birds and tiny, timid
mammals. Some early reptiles
brooded and protected their young,
making them among the world's
first caring parents.

EARLY HUMANS

Our ancestors, the first modern
humans, appeared about 300,000
years ago, a very recent chapter in
the history of the universe.

A World of Wonders

Have you ever gone outside in the dark and gazed up at the starry night sky? Did it make you wonder how you came to be here, a part of this shining universe?

The Universe Began With a Bang

The universe is so old that no one was around to see how it began. But after studying space with powerful telescopes, looking for clues, scientists have come to a surprising conclusion. They think that everything in existence was originally squished into an extremely tiny, extremely heavy ball. About 13.8 billion years ago, that little dot-of-everything suddenly burst open and began expanding, faster than the speed of light, in every direction. This colossal explosion is often called the Big Bang.

For the first hundred million years or so, the early universe was dark and filled with a kind of thick, hot soup. As this soup slowly cooled, it turned into swirling clouds and clumps of gases and dust, drawn together by a force called gravity. The more tightly the clumps were held together, the hotter they became, until—all of a sudden—some of them began to glow. The first stars had been born.

The early stars were huge, many times larger than our Sun. Inside their fierce, flaming cores, they reworked the matter that had been released by the Big Bang into new forms, or elements, like calcium and iron. After a few million years, the giant stars exploded, sending gusts of element-rich dust into the cosmos. The dust was pulled together by gravity to form new stars, which blazed and exploded in turn.

Over time, the building blocks for everything that exists today were created inside stars. That includes you. You are made of star stuff, too.

Meanwhile, gravity continued its work, gathering stars together in clusters called galaxies. Planets, including Earth, formed when bits of space debris crashed into each other, stuck together, and began to orbit around some of those countless stars. Scientists estimate that the universe contains as many as two trillion galaxies, each made up of a hundred million stars that are circled by a hundred million worlds. It is enough to send our minds spinning with wonder.

Life on Earth

Of all the billions and trillions of planets in the universe, only one is known to support life. That miraculous world is our home, the Earth.

The Earth formed about 4.6 billion years ago as a sizzling hot mass of cosmic debris. As the planet cooled, its surface solidified into rock, and water began to pool in lakes and oceans. In addition, new arrivals from space—comets and other small objects—crash-landed on Earth, delivering more water and more building blocks for life.

After a very long time, these building blocks combined to form proteins and other molecules, which became part of simple living things. Over millions and millions of years— through countless strange successes and spectacular failures—life evolved in a dazzling parade of wild and wonderful forms. Our own ancestors, the first modern humans, appeared about 300,000 years ago.

And here is what is truly amazing: Everything that has happened, from the Big Bang to this very moment, has led to YOU. The story of the universe is your story.

Candace Savage is the award-winning author of more than two dozen books, many of which reflect her love of the living world. Her writing for young people has been honored by the Canadian Children's Book Centre and the New York Public Library, among others. In 2022, she received both the Cheryl and Henry Kloppenburg Award for Literary Excellence and the Matt Cohen Award: In Celebration of a Writing Life. She is privileged to live and write in Treaty Six territory and the homeland of the Métis Nation in Saskatchewan, Canada.

Rachel Wada is a freelance illustrator based in Vancouver, BC. Her visual style is an amalgamation of cultural influences and techniques that reflect her Japanese-Chinese heritage. Rachel creates illustrations for children's books, magazines, advertising campaigns, murals, and more. She draws inspiration from the everyday and finds joy in visually communicating thoughts, emotions and ideas that are often intangible. Rachel loves incorporating lots of texture and vibrant colors in her work to amplify the emotional undertones of stories and ideas big and small.